A MAN DIES BUT ONCE

MATTHEW HARFFY

Cover design: Gareth Jones

www.matthewharffy.com

This novella is set in 19th century Texas and reflects the realities of that time and place, including historical language, attitudes, violence and depictions of enslaved people.

ONE

A man always remembers his first murder. Just like he always remembers his first visit to the whore house. I've killed more men than I can rightly recall. Back in eighty or eighty-one down Tombstone way, a fat, sweaty newspaper man asked me how many hombres I'd put in the ground. I chewed my quid of tobacco for a spell, running through them in my head. After a time, I aimed a hunk of weed juice at the brass spittoon by the door. I missed and some of the liquid splattered on the writer's shoe. He looked down in disgust, but did not comment.

"Well," I said, "it's more than twenty. But I got all turned around in my head after that and lost count."

"D'you tally Indians in that number?" The fat man was breathless. He pulled a white handkerchief from his pocket and mopped his brow. Then he looked down at the brown drops on his shoe, but evidently decided against wiping them off with the small, pale square of cotton.

I spat again and this time hit the spittoon with a satisfying plop. The sweaty man flinched.

"Of course that don't include Indians," I said. "Mexicans neither. No self-respecting man I've ever known tallies bean eaters or redskins."

The truth was I took no man lightly when it came to a fight.

A Mexican ball or Comanche arrow will kill you just as sure as a Texan bullet. But I had a reputation to maintain.

Since then, I've forgotten a whole passel of men who've passed in their chips after crossing me.

But I'll never forget killing Larry Woodrow, just like I'll never forget my first poke with sweet Pearl McCall. She's dead now too. She got taken by the consumption not a year after I first laid eyes on her. I was smitten, as boys of sixteen will be by a pretty Angelica with skin so lily-white you could almost see through it on a bright day. From the moment I saw her standing in the shade outside old Brent's saloon, I'd burnt for her, thinking of what lay under her frilly skirts and what it would be like to touch that soft, pale skin.

When it came to those two firsts, the killing and the poking, both crept up on me as a surprise and were over in not much more than the blink of an eye. And I dare say neither Larry nor Pearl were much impressed by the experience. With Pearl I got to practice a bunch more times, and I got a mite better at the poking, though I've never been anything special in that regard. For Larry, there was no second time. A man dies but once, and it turned out that, unlike with the poking, I was a natural at killing.

TWO

I have witnessed all manner of events that stay with a man, but I recall that day as clearly as any in my life. I was riding the buckskin, Buttermilk, Pa had given me on my thirteenth birthday and Sam ran along behind in the dust kicked up by the horse's hooves. Sam was a rangy scruff of a collie who looked more wild animal than pet. He'd wandered onto the farm one day when he must have only been a few months old. Ma had found him curled up on the porch one morning when she opened the door to sweep out the grit and dust that was ever blowing in. She did her best to keep our home as clean and tidy as the house where she had grown up back east. It was an impossible task, but that didn't stop Ma, and woe betide anyone who did not scrape the mud from his boots before entering.

Pa didn't want us to keep the dog, but Jacob, Beryl and I pleaded with him until he relented.

"Well, I sure as Sam Hill, ain't feeding the mutt," he'd snarled, and the name stuck. In time, Pa grew to grudgingly appreciate Sam, who more than once warned us of the presence of men and beasts who might do harm to our stock. He was never a house dog. He slept outside in all weathers, but I took to feeding him morsels from my plate after each meal. My brother and sister both grew weary of the puppy with his sharp teeth, but despite the needling scratches on my ankles, I rushed outside each morning with scraps for Sam and we became inseparable. He could keep up with a horse at a gallop and never seemed to tire.

I had ridden out early that morning, just as the sun hazed the eastern horizon. The air was clear and the land smelt as fresh as if God had just made it, damp with the dew that would soon be burnt away by the hot sun. Ma was already awake and stood by the stove beating up batter.

"Where are you headed so early?" she asked.

"Gonna check the head up in the high pasture," I lied.

"Biscuits will be ready soon."

"I won't wait," I said. "It's a long way out past the butte." This was true, but Ma gave me a sidelong look. I was not one to pass up a meal, especially not Ma's biscuits. The thought of them made my mouth water, but I could not wait. The ride to Collado Springs was even further than the high pasture. "I don't want to be caught out after dark," I added, knowing that would do the trick. Ma had not grown up on the ranch and she still held a city girl's fear of the darkness. She imagined savages and coyotes lurking behind every tree, though any Indians who wished to make war on the whites had long-since left these lands behind. There were still plenty of Comanches and Apaches who would have scalped us, and done worse to Ma and Beryl, in a heartbeat, but there were safer places for them to raid, and Indians ain't stupid. There were too many guns around town, so they didn't bother us none.

"You be careful," she said, bringing me a slice of the pie we'd had the night before.

"I always am," I said with a grin, my breath steaming in the cool dawn. "You know me."

"That's what I'm afraid of," she said, as I swung up into the saddle and spurred Buttermilk southward, our long shadows bumping along the ground beside us.

If she had known where I was headed, she would have been more worried. She thought I was riding into the hills that, in her mind at least, were infested with redskins and wild animals.

There was only one thing Ma feared more than the wilderness, and that was the nearby settlement of Collado Springs. As soon as I was out of sight of the house, I turned towards the northwest and set Buttermilk to an easy lope that would carry me to my destination by midday.

THREE

I was only a boy, and had seen next to nothing of the world, so it was natural some of her fear had rubbed off on me. I rode into town with some trepidation. After the quiet of the open land, the sounds and sights of the bustling street sent my head spinning. Ma often spoke in reverential tones about her youth in Richmond, how she loved walking in the shade of the grand buildings of Capitol Square, and perusing the latest fashions from Europe in the shops that lined Cary Street. It seemed strange to me that she should find the tiny town of Collado Springs so unwelcoming. Surely it was a smaller version of her beloved Richmond and every great city had to start somewhere.

Collado Springs seemed to have grown even in the few weeks since I'd last visited with Pa to pick up supplies from Hyslop's. A couple of houses had sprung up on the south side of town, there were several tents to the north, and the frame of a large building, that would end up being the Grand Hotel, loomed at the end of Main Street, surrounded by laborers, shouting, cussing and laughing as they hammered and sawed at the timber.

I rode past the blacksmith and the ringing of metal on metal. It was a warm day, and I could barely imagine the discomfort of working at the forge, but there was the ruddy-faced smith,

6

hammering away at the glowing metal. A line of horses was hitched outside the livery stable awaiting their new shoes. I recognized the brand on the animals as belonging to the Triple Circle spread. It must have been pay day, when the cowhands would descend on the town to spend their cash money. I hadn't realized it was the last day of the month, and felt a tremor of unease at knowing that the town that Ma described as like "Sodom and Gomorrah" at the best of times would be even busier and filled with cowboys eager to let off steam after weeks of working the range.

As if to underline my thoughts, a young man in leather overalls and a wide-brimmed hat stumbled backwards into my path. He sprawled onto his back in the dirt, losing his high-crowned hat in the process, to expose a prematurely balding head. Buttermilk reared, almost toppling me from the saddle, but I managed to cling on to the pommel. Sam snarled at the man, as he leapt to his feet. Ignoring the dog, he pulled a large knife from his belt.

"I'm gonna gut you like a hog," he said, his words slurred and fuzzy from drink even though it was barely noon.

Another cowboy, face flushed and eyes gleaming beneath his dark hat, stepped down from the sidewalk, big Mexican spurs jangling. His hands were empty and he held them up to show as much.

"Think twice before waving that knife at me," he said. "I'll whip you right here and now if you ain't ready to take back what you said. But I ain't heeled, so drop the knife. I'll kill you if you try and cut me up."

Several other cowpunchers were watching the altercation, and a few called out, some offering support of the knife-wielding man, others siding with the unarmed hand.

The big knife glinted in the balding man's hand as he swayed where he stood. His eyes flickered left and right, taking in the onlookers. He was clearly unsure what he should do. To back down now would be to lose face, but his adversary had a cold stillness about him that spoke of danger.

"Put it away, Slim," snapped a stocky man from the other

side of the street where he had been perusing the wares outside Grafton's Mercantile and Sundries. His voice cut through the shouts and taunts of the unruly cowhands. He was not a tall man, but as they say, size doesn't matter, and the authority in his tone was clear as a bell.

I recognized him as Buck Burnett, foreman of the Triple Circle ranch.

The man with the knife glanced at him, then, swallowing, he sheathed the blade.

"I've no need for a knife to lick the likes of you," he growled, and in the same instant swung a clumsy punch, hoping to catch the other man off guard.

Without a word, the man in the dark hat stepped forward quickly, catching the blow on his left forearm and hammering a straight right into Slim's jaw. Slim, staggered back a pace, then sat down hard, his eyes glazed and blinking.

The quiet man looked at Slim, sitting in the dust. Disdain was clear on his face.

"Keep him away from me until he's sober," he said. "If he wants to make a thing out of this, then I'll meet him outside of town tomorrow."

Turning on his heel, he stepped back onto the boardwalk and walked away, deciding Slim was no longer a threat.

Burnett it seemed was not so sure. He made his way over to where some of the ranch hands were helping Slim to his feet and without pausing, he plucked the knife from its sheath.

"I'll leave this at the sheriff's office. You can pick it up with your gun when you leave town." Slim shook his head and frowned. He looked ready to protest when Burnett went on, addressing Slim's friends. "See to it he doesn't get his hands on any other weapon. If there's trouble, I'll hold you all responsible."

This threat seemed to throw water on their fire, and they sloped off like scolded children.

Moving back across the road to the shade in front of Grafton's, Burnett seemed to notice me for the first time, sitting astride Buttermilk, watching the proceedings.

8

"Their sap is up, Jed," he said, squinting up at me from beneath the brim of his hat. You'd best get whatever it is your pa sent you for and then skedaddle. The boys have money in their pockets and are only like to get rowdier as the day goes on. And if anything should befall you, your mother would blame me and have me flayed alive."

The thought of my Ma whipping Buck Burnett tickled me, and I couldn't help smiling. I didn't even know they were acquainted. At the time I didn't give it much thought, but years later, looking back with the eyes of an older man, I realize my mother was a handsome woman in a land of rough men. Of course, they all knew her. I suspect a few were hoping Pa might have an accident before she got too old to make a good wife.

"Go on now, hurry along," Burnett said, stepping into the shadow of the store.

I touched my heels to Buttermilk and trotted down the street towards Brent's. Just like the boys from the Triple Circle, I too had money. More money than I had ever had before. It was burning a hole in my pocket like a hot coal. And there was only one thing I wanted to spend it on. My waking thoughts and dreams had been filled with visions of Pearl for weeks, but I had not truly believed I would ever have enough money to partake of her services. Not for years anyway. I was innocent and young, but I was no fool. I knew she was a girl of the line, and I never had more than a couple of bits to my name. Pa didn't pay me for my chores. I had little idea how much the ladies at Brent's Saloon charged, but I was pretty certain it would be more than a quarter. And so, I had resigned myself to yearning and dreaming.

That had changed a couple of nights before when I had followed Jacob to the bunkhouse. My older brother liked to play cards with the ranch hands and he had finally agreed to allow me to join them. If Ma found out we'd been gambling with the men, there would have been hell to pay, but neither Jacob nor I were dumb enough to tell her, and we knew better than to let Beryl know. We had learnt the hard way that our sister was incapable of keeping a secret.

I'd been excited to sit down with the tough vaqueros who worked our small ranch. They had dealt me in with grins and chuckles, sure they were going to do me out of my scant savings in no time. Their smiles vanished soon enough though. Turns out having a cool head and a quick mind means I am passing good at cards.

That was a year of several firsts for me. On the verge of becoming a man and I learnt I could outplay most anyone at cards. I've won many a hand of poker over the years, and even raked in a pot of more than two thousand dollars once in Cheyenne. I've played so many games of chance I lost count, but like with the other firsts that came that year, I have never forgotten the pot I won in that gloomy bunkhouse that stank of leather, sweat, tobacco and horses.

By the end of the night, I had close to five dollars in my pile of winnings. None of it was paper money, and I had never seen so many coins all in one place. And right then, as I counted my money, I started to formulate the plan to visit Pearl. I was too embarrassed to ask any of the hands how much it might cost to spend time with one of the girls I'd heard them refer to as Mauks, but I hoped I would have enough. The cowprods grumbled that I must have been cheating, which got me fired up angry. In all my years I never saw the need for cheating, but I've had to kill men who accused me of such. And I've drilled a few men I caught with cards up their sleeves. But I was a boy then, so I swallowed my anger and did my best to ignore the men who'd lost to me. They wanted to play the next night to win back their money. I refused. I daren't lose the key that might open the door to Miss Pearl's boudoir.

I jumped down from Buttermilk outside Brent's Saloon. It was full, and the sound of men talking, laughing, and shouting rolled out of the open door on a cloud of tobacco smoke. There were a dozen horses hitched to the rail and I jostled a couple out of the way so that I could tie Buttermilk where he could drink from the trough that still had some water in it. A paint mustang snapped at Buttermilk, but the buckskin whinnied and showed his teeth and the mustang gave him room.

Stepping up onto the wooden walkway outside the saloon, I was suddenly nervous. A piece of paper nailed to the wall beside the entrance stated that no firearms were permitted within the city limits. These flyers were all over Collado Springs. A sudden roaring of laughter tumbled out of the saloon. With a shock, I realized what was missing from the sounds I was used to hearing coming from the cavernous interior of Brent's: piano music. Brent had employed a dapper-looking man called Pierre to play the piano. A few weeks prior, a drunken teamster, apparently not a lover of the arts, pulled out an old Allen pepperbox pistol and shot Pierre dead. News of the shooting had only served to reinforce my mother's fear of town and it was this most recent killing that had led to the ban on firearms.

"You going in or out?" asked a voice close beside me. I jumped like a snake-bit horse and I felt my face grow hot.

It was the man with the dark hat. A half dozen cowboys were with him. They were broad-shouldered, strong men, with moustaches and whiskers, and skin like leather from the wind and sun of the range. They were all looking at me and my embarrassment grew.

"Well? Which is it?"

I blinked stupidly.

"In or out?" asked the man, his fraying patience noticeable in his tone. "You're blocking the door, boy, and the daylight's burning."

I swallowed. I had never set foot inside a bar before. All I had heard about them were tales of drunkenness, gambling, fighting, and whores. I had seen this man fighting just moments before. I had acquired a taste for gambling already, and I had come for one of the whores, so perhaps saloons weren't so bad after all, I reasoned. Anyhow, I'd come too far to turn around now. I puffed out my chest and stepped inside.

Sam followed me, and the cowboys came behind, swarming into the dark interior.

"No dogs in here!" shouted the grizzled barman from the back of the saloon.

One of the cowboys laughed.

"Yeah, smells enough already in here without hounds shitting all over the place."

"If you don't like it, O'Leary," growled the barkeep, "you can always get yourself down to Grafton's."

Grafton sold supplies, and also served beer and whiskey in a side room, but there was no gambling and no whores in his place. Neither establishment had music now, but apparently that was not what attracted most men in to spend their tin. O'Leary, clearly deciding he would rather stay put, shut his mouth and sidled sheepishly up to the bar.

"I was only joshing with you," he said.

The barman looked like he'd sat on a prickly pear, but said nothing further. Reaching for glasses, he uncorked a bottle and filled one for each of the newcomers.

"You still there?" he shouted over at me without warning. "I told you to get your mutt out of here."

The cowhands laughed and several faces turned in my direction.

"Come on, Sam," I whispered, backing out into the street once more.

I scanned the sidewalk for somewhere to tie him. The horses nickered and the paint horse that had taken a bite at Buttermilk rolled its eyes and kicked out at Sam. Fearing he might get trampled if I tied him to the hitching rail, I walked around the corner, where there was a yard, a storage hut, and a side entrance into the saloon's kitchen. It would be quieter there, I thought, away from the scurry and rush of the street.

I whistled for Sam to follow me, and he obediently padded along at my heels. As I rounded the corner a man's raucous shouting hit me like a slap.

"Come on, boy! I ain't got all day!"

A wagon was parked there, still hitched to a team of mules that were dusty and sweat-lathered. My Pa would have told the owner to get the beasts curried and cleaned. He had no time for a man who mistreats his animals, though it is all too common an occurrence in this world of ours.

An ugly man was leaning against one of the wagon's wheels.

He had a torn hat and a long straggly beard that looked as if mice might be nesting in it.

"Don't pretend that's heavy, you good for nothing devil!" he yelled. "If you don't show lively, I'll be taking my whip to you. You know I ain't lying."

To the rear of the wagon, a black skinned African man, stripped to the waste and gleaming with sweat, labored under the weight of a barrel. As I watched, he heaved it onto his shoulder and shuffled towards the door of the saloon. He didn't raise his eyes to look at me or Sam, and he appeared not to hear the man's shouting. As he set his burden down, I saw his back was criss-crossed with a latticework of raised scars.

"What you staring at, boy?"

The man's tone was sharp, bitter and spiny as tree cholla. His voice made my skin crawl.

"Nothing," I mumbled. "Just tying up my dog." I wasn't too keen on leaving Sam there with the bearded man, but my desire for Pearl was building now that I was so close to my goal. I had ridden all this way, taken the first step into the saloon. My plan was so near to falling into place that I could barely stand it. My mind was fogged with thoughts of Pearl's pale skin in the way only a sixteen-year-old boy's mind can become addled by thoughts of the fairer sex.

"Pay no heed to Hannibal," the man said, mistaking my unease. "He won't hurt you. Go ahead and tie up your dog." He offered me a grin that showed a mouthful of brown teeth. Reaching up to the wagon driver's seat, he retrieved a bottle of whiskey and took a swig. "Name's Woodrow. Larry Woodrow. What do they call you, kid?"

The negro looked at me for the first time, eyes hooded, sweat-bejeweled face expressionless. For a moment my eyes lingered on the scars that spoke of the harsh treatment he'd suffered and I thought of Pa again, and how he would not stand for a man mistreating his beasts of burden.

"Jed," I mumbled, not wishing to speak with the teamster any longer than I had to.

A woman's laughter drifted from a small window and my

thoughts returned to Pearl and the pang of longing I felt for her.

I pulled a length of hemp string from my pocket. Unsheathing the hunting knife I wore on my belt, I cut the cord so that there would be enough for a leash. Looping the string around Sam's neck, I quickly secured him to a piece of fencing. Sam hated to be tied, but he lay down in the slice of shadow there.

"Don't worry, kid," said Woodrow. "I'll watch him for ya."

I muttered my thanks and hurried back to the front of the saloon and what I hoped awaited me inside. Sam eyed me balefully as I left.

FOUR

As soon as I was back inside the cool shadow of the saloon, I hesitated. I had no clue what to do next. I scanned the interior, searching for the object of my desire, but Pearl was nowhere to be seen. The cowboys who had come in with me were still standing at the bar, glasses in their hands. Off to my right there was a table running a game of Faro. There were four men betting and speaking loudly to the dealer, who was turning over cards with a flourish as if he was doing magic tricks. I didn't know how to play the game, but my recent success at poker made me think that perhaps the Faro table might be the place to start my quest.

Before I could make my way towards the game, a rippling of feminine laughter pulled my attention away. On the other side of the room, sitting with her back to the silent piano, sat a woman. My heart lurched before I saw this was not my Pearl. This strumpet was plump and old to my young gaze. The skin of her face was pocked and smeared with thick rouge, and her gaudy dress was hitched up to expose her dimpled flabby thighs that reminded me of the bread dough Ma would punch and stretch on the kitchen table back home.

A sinewy man in a dark suit and a small round-crowned hat was sitting with the woman. He was whispering to her, leaning forward, his hand sliding up the white skin of her leg.

I had never seen so much of a lady's leg on display. The pale flesh captivated me, and I craned my neck till it hurt, unable to look away as I moved like a somnambulist towards the bar.

"What do you want?"

The grey-haired barman's gruff voice dragged me away from the woman's meaty thighs.

"Huh?"

I had momentarily forgotten how to speak.

Beside me, from where he was standing with his back against the bar, the black-hatted cowhand chuckled.

"You simple, boy?" he asked.

I looked at him, confusion clear on my face.

"You came into this here saloon with a purpose. As far as I see it, there are only three reasons that might have brought you here. Whiskey, Faro, or the Calico Queens. By the way your eyes are bulgin' staring at Sally's nether regions, I'd say we know which one you are after, eh, boys?"

The other men laughed and I felt myself blush.

"You wait your turn," slurred the man with the woman called Sally. His hand had disappeared all the way up under her skirt now. His eyes shone and his cheeks were red, but Sally appeared bored.

"Don't you worry, honey," she said, her voice musical and tender in a way that reminded me of Ma. "This one won't take long at all and then I'll be happy to spend some time with you."

Flustered, I briskly turned my back on her. My thoughts were all of a muddle. I could feel my pizzle stirring in my pants at the sight of the cowboy's hand slipping up Sally's leg, but the sound of her voice, so like Ma's, made me shudder.

The men at the bar were smiling at my discomfiture. I didn't know what to say and I started thinking this was all a big mistake. If Pa should find out I didn't ride to the high pasture, he'd tan my hide. And if Ma heard I'd visited the saloon, I could barely begin to imagine how mad she would be.

"Well?" asked the barkeep, his tone tired, as if he'd seen all of this play out a hundred times before. "What'll it be?"

"Whiskey," I blurted out. I don't rightly know what got into me that day. I could have asked for a seltzer, ginger ale, or a coffee. Hell, I could even have ordered a beer. Instead, I went for another first. On Ma's insistence, Pa had taken the pledge, so didn't allow any alcoholic beverage in the house. I had never tasted whiskey, so I was in no way prepared for the burning rawness as I tossed the liquid into my mouth the way I had seen the cowpokes do.

I spluttered and coughed. The men laughed again, and even the sullen barman cracked a smile. I had asked for the drink to distract from the embarrassment of them thinking I was there for a poke with Sally, but instead I had embarrassed myself even further. I was a boy acting the part of a man, and they all knew it. My cheeks burnt as the man in the black hat slapped me on the back.

"Two bits," said the barman, uncaring for my discomfort.

I could scarce believe it was such a price for the rotgut that still burnt my throat. I didn't know if I was being taken for a ride, but none of the men at the bar commented, so I fished out a handful of coins from my pocket, found a quarter, and slapped it down on the wet bartop with as much confidence as I could muster.

I had just about got my breath back. I could still feel the firewater searing down inside me on its way to my stomach. I reckoned I would be able to keep it down, but I was glad I had swallowed it quickly. I didn't suppose any man could bare to sip the stuff. In fact, I could scarce understand why anyone would drink liquor for pleasure. It was all I could do not to gag. Then, to my dismay, the man beside me took the bottle that rested before him, pulled out the cork and poured a sizeable glug into my glass. He filled his own and clinked his against mine in a friendly way. He was grinning.

"Name's Gordon Sage," he said. "Good to see a man who can take his drink." He raised his glass, and there was nothing for it but to do likewise. "What do they call you?"

The vapors from the liquor assaulted my nose and the thought of drinking more whiskey made my belly ache. The bottle was being passed down the bar and his pals were all filling their glasses.

"Jed," I muttered.

"Well, Jed," he said with a smile, his teeth white in his darkly weathered face, "here's to new friends."

"To new friends," shouted his ranch buddies, and as one, they drained their glasses.

Sage's eyes never left mine as he drank. I hesitated for a second, then lifted the glass to my lips.

The liquor didn't burn quite as much the second time round and when I had emptied my glass, I slammed it down onto the bar, emulating the men. Sage reached for the bottle and, seeing it was empty, he held it up.

"Another," he said in a cheery voice to the barman.

My heart sank at the thought of having to drink more and my mind whirled, trying to think of ways to escape this situation. Ma was right. I should never have come here. The whiskey was making me sick and I was already starting to feel woozy. Now, after years of practice, I can drink from dawn to sundown and still be sharp enough to beat most men at cards, but this was my first taste of what Ma called the "demon drink" and my guts were churning.

The barman produced another bottle and placed it down in front of us.

"Two dollars," he said.

I didn't move, but Sage clapped me on the back.

"That's mighty decent of you, Jed."

He had one hand on the bar and my eyes were drawn to his knuckles. They were red and the skin was split from where he had clouted Slim. I could feel the eyes of the other Triple Circle cowhands on me, perhaps anticipating a ruckus if I refused to pay. My heart sank. I'd only had about five dollars when I rode into town. At this rate, by the time I saw Pearl I would be as poor as I had been before my unexpected wins at poker. But I could see no way out of this. Sage had given me some of his whiskey, now I had to return the favor. I pulled out a handful of specie and counted out two dollars. The barman sniffed and scooped the coins off the bar.

Sage hadn't waited for me to complete the transaction before uncorking the bottle and filling everyone's glasses. He raised his to me, then threw back his head, swallowing the contents. His eyes were bright. With a resigned sigh, I copied him. I was ready for the taste and fire of the whiskey now, and I did not gag. My whole body was warm now, and everything had begun to feel soft around the edges.

"So what brings you to town?" Sage asked.

Part of me wanted to tell this stranger all about Pearl and my burning desire for her. Surely he would know what I needed to do to see her. But I hadn't drunk enough whiskey yet to completely unburden myself. I hadn't told anybody how I felt, not even Jacob.

"Pa sent me in for some supplies," I lied vaguely.

"Is that so?" His expression told me he did not believe me for a second. "Hardened drinker are you?" He grinned at the obvious absurdity of his words, given my reaction to my first taste of liquor. I was as comfortable in that bar as a catfish is on a horse.

"What?" I asked, feeling stupid. The world tilted around me. I placed a hand on the bar to steady myself. "Why d'ya say that?"

"Saw you ride straight here after you arrived. You rode up right after I was done having words with Slim Denby."

I felt foolish, so decided to change the subject away from me and my habits.

"What did he say to you to get you so riled up?"

He refilled his glass, but left mine empty this time.

"Riled up, you say?" He shook his head and smiled. "Jed, if I were truly riled, Denby would be getting measured for a coffin right now. No, he's just a mean drunk. Tomorrow he'll say sorry and all will be forgiven." There was a hardness about Gordon Sage that made me doubt he was a forgiving man, but I did not press the issue. "Now, before you go about your chores in town, what say you we put some of your Pa's money to good use?"

I was confused for a moment, until I saw where he was looking. There were more men around the Faro table now and the flamboyant dealer was calling out the winners as he laid the cards. As I've said, I'd never played before, but even back then, I felt the call of the cards. I've been a sporting man all my life since, and I've spent more hours betting and playing cards than I could begin to count. But as a sixteen-year-old, the allure of a pretty woman was stronger than almost anything else on God's great earth. I wanted to see what Faro was like to play, but I was terrified I would lose the rest of my money, making my journey to Collado Springs pointless. And the Lord only knew when I might again get the chance to come alone with money to spend.

I was about to make some excuse for why I couldn't play, when a series of whistles and catcalls filled the saloon. The men at the Faro table turned around to see what was the cause of the commotion. The cowhands at the bar were all hollering and staring too. I turned quickly, holding on to the bar to prevent myself from losing my balance. I'd only had three drams of liquor, but it seemed to me that the floor in Brent's had become a mite unstable.

A young man was coming down the stairs at the rear of the large room. His hat was in his hand and his suspenders hung loose from his pants. As he reached the bottom step, he hooked the suspenders under his thumb and looped them over his shoulder. Waving his hat in the air like a man breaking in a bronc, he grinned at the cowhands by the bar. They returned his wave with a cheer, as if welcoming back a conquering hero.

My breath caught in my throat as I saw the slight figure who descended the stairs behind him. Pearl was even prettier than I recalled. Her cheeks were pink as if she had just come in from riding at a gallop, which, thinking 'bout it now, I suppose she had, in a manner of speaking. Her hair was loose, its curls gleaming in a cascade that tumbled over her shoulders. She swept the room with her gaze and with a thrill, I was sure her eyes settled on me for a moment. My young heart swelled in my chest and suddenly I was once again glad I had ridden all that way. Nothing else mattered apart from getting to spend time with this vision of beauty.

The smiling cowhand pushed his hat back on his head and swaggered over to the bar. I ignored him, unable to take my eyes off Pearl.

Beside me, Gordon Sage whistled.

"So that's the real reason you're in town, eh, pard?" he said, slapping me on the shoulder. I did not deny it. There was no point. My hopeless infatuation was written on my face, plain for all to see as clearly as if it had been printed on one of the sheriff's flyers. "Hey, Pearl," Sage went on, "fancy a whiskey?"

My face burnt as she walked towards us. I could not look away from the sway of her hips and how her skirts swished around her shapely ankles.

"Just a small one then," she said. Her voice had the lilt of the south-east, Georgia perhaps. "It's going to be a long day."

"I doubt it will be long with this one," Sage said, nodding to indicate me. The cowboys all laughed. My face burnt hotter, though to tell the truth, I didn't rightly know what they meant.

Pearl looked me up and down. My mouth grew drier than a bag of flour and I wondered whether I shouldn't take another mouthful of whiskey.

"You came to see me?" she asked, smiling softly. She had a confidence about her I could only dream of. I have no idea of her age. She couldn't have been any older than twenty-one or two, but she spoke with the ease of someone who knows they command the room.

I nodded, unable to speak. She accepted a glass of whiskey from Gordon and sipped delicately at the golden-brown liquid.

"You can thank Jed here for the drink," Sage said.

"Handsome and generous," she replied. She knew her business, and was used to the rough, drunk men who came in from the land. It was no difficulty for her to wrap me around her finger with a couple of words and a smile. Jeez, she didn't even need to speak. I was smitten by her before she walked down the stairs.

She took another sip of whiskey.

"Thanks for the drink, honey."

"You're welcome," I muttered, glad then I'd been duped into buying the bottle. The thought of the cost of the whiskey made me suddenly anxious. "I'm not sure... That is to say..." My words trailed off. Like stepping up to saddle an unbroken mustang, I wasn't sure how to approach the subject of money with her.

She reached out and stroked the back of my hand with her long, pale fingers. They were cool to the touch.

"What is it, sugar? No need to be nervous."

Her touch inflamed me. I shifted my stance, uncomfortably aware that my pizzle was stiffening in my pants. I could sense all the cowhands leaning in to hear what I was gonna say and I worried they might see my state of arousal. All of this was embarrassing enough, without an audience. But I had come this far, and if I got what I craved from Pearl, this was surely not going to be the most embarrassing thing I would do that day.

"I'm not certain—" My voice cracked in my suddenly dry throat. Picking up the bottle, I poured a splash of whiskey into my empty glass, not stopping to think how easily I turned to the drink for help. Knocking back the liquor, I tried again. "I am not certain how much it costs to..." I hesitated, unsure how to proceed.

"To spend some time with me?" she concluded for me.

I nodded, thankfully.

"How much do you have?"

I pulled out the coins from my pocket and spread them on the counter. She brushed her fingers over the metal, quickly tallying up the total value.

"What's he got?" said a voice from the top of the stairs.

I hadn't noticed anyone there, so consumed had I been with Pearl. Now I peered into the shadows on the landing and saw there was an older woman seated there. I learnt in that moment to always make sure to look up and in the shadows when I enter a place. I know more than one man who's been shot by someone they would have otherwise noticed had they been paying more attention to their surroundings.

"Just shy of three dollars," said Pearl.

The woman on the landing shook her head.

"Can't go lower than four."

"Hey," shouted one of the cowhands, a tall man with long hair and a buckskin shirt, "you charge me five. What makes this kid so special?"

Special? I didn't feel special. I felt like a fool. I had come with enough money, and spent it buying whiskey for strangers. Now I wouldn't be able to fulfil the goal of my quest. Perhaps I could win some more money at the Faro table, I mused, the pull of the game singing to me the way they say sirens used to sing to sailors, calling them to their doom.

"I'm minded to give a discount for a boy's first time," said the woman in reply to the cowhand. I chose not to ask how she knew it was my first time, guessing my lack of experience was evident.

"Besides, Tom," said Pearl in a sweet voice, "you're a real handful. You tire a girl out. It's only fair you pay a bit extra for all the effort."

His friends guffawed and clapped. The tall man appeared mollified by her words.

"That's why she charged me six dollars!" said the man who had so recently come down from Pearl's room on the second floor.

"No, Frank," said Sage, his eyes twinkling, "she charges you extra for the smell. I told you to have a bath first."

Everyone laughed, including Pearl and Frank, who didn't appear to take any offence at Sage's words. I didn't join in with the merriment. I felt a stab of envy as I realized that she had just spent time with this cowboy. The thought of it made me angry, even though I knew her profession. She had probably been with all of those buckaroos. They certainly all seemed to know her. But standing there, so close to her that I could detect the scent of her rose perfume and the muskier smell of her skin, the idea of her allowing anyone other than me to touch her, drove me crazy with jealousy.

Still, it was no matter. I didn't have the money to pay her.

Unless I could win at Faro, I would be forced to ride back home without having done that which I had come for. I had burnt for her before, her image filling my dreams and thoughts, but now that she had spoken to me and touched my hand. Now that I had smelt her aroma, I didn't think I would be able to sleep again.

The whiskey was still working in me, and I swayed on my feet. Such was my disappointment that I could feel tears prickling my eyes. I sniffed, and looked down. To cry in front of these men and Pearl would be more than I could bear. I would never be able to show my face in the saloon again. I had come here on a man's purpose. I could not weep like a boy. But the whiskey appeared to heighten my emotions, and I felt that tears were imminent and I would not be able to halt them if I started crying.

To my surprise, Gordon Sage clasped my shoulder.

"Don't worry, pard," he said, his tone softer than it had been up to this point. "Thanks for the whiskey." Without a further word, he produced two shining dollar coins from his jacket pocket and handed them to me.

The coins glimmered, cold and hard in my hand. I had been furious a moment before, feeling that he'd bullied me into parting with my money, leaving me unable to go upstairs with Pearl.

"I— You—" I stammered. I struggled to find the right words. In the end I settled on: "Thank you."

He winked.

"What are friends for?"

I passed the coins to Pearl, who hid them away inside her dress. She counted off another two dollars' worth from the coins on the bar, then took my hand.

The touch of her fingers against my palm sent a shock through my body, like I'd been struck by lightning.

The cowboys whistled and jeered as if I was one of their own. I didn't turn back as she led me up the stairs.

FIVE

Pearl's room was small, but clean and tidy. The bed was made, covered in a pink counterpane. There was a simple chair in the corner, a sprig of bluebonnets and blackfoot daisies in a tiny vase on the dresser. There were even lacy curtains hanging over the window. I now know such things are not common in a whore's crib. You have to pay a darn sight more than four dollars to get clean sheets along with your poke. Once, when I was flush from the gold mining camps of Grass Valley, I spent a whole week living in a brothel in San Francisco where the madame had tiny Chinese women come in and change the sheets for freshly starched linen after every customer. I was rich when I arrived, but poor when I left. But not once have I regretted my stay there, nor do I begrudge the cost. I never did have that sort of ballast again, so I ain't tasted such luxury in my life since.

But Brent's was a small saloon in a cattle town on the edge of the prairie, and I have never since known a trug's room in such an establishment to be anything but dingy and unkempt. I cannot say I blame the soiled doves for living in squalor. They have a constant procession of men traipsing through messing things up. Dusty cowhands, muddy farmers, drunken businessmen, even lonely townsmen, who might be clean yet

25

MATTHEW HARFFY

embarrassed to be there. But they all bring their muck with them, and leave without sparing a thought for the man who follows them.

Despite the tidiness, I could detect the tang of horse, sweat and leather that lingered in the room; a sour reminder that not ten minutes prior Pearl had been lying with the cowboy from the Triple Circle.

I looked at the bed and stood awkwardly by the closed door. The sounds of chatter from the bar below were muted, but still loud through the thin pine.

I watched Pearl as she made her way to the window and tugged it open. The curtains billowed in with the breeze, fluttering over her face for a moment like a wedding veil.

"It's getting warm in here," she said, brushing the curtain away and turning back to face me. The light caught in her hair, and showed off the curve of her breast.

I could barely catch my breath. We had not spoken since she had grasped my hand. I'd followed her silently, my heart hammering fit to burst in my chest, my pecker so hard I thought it must rip through the cotton of my pants. It throbbed painfully with each surge of my racing blood.

She smiled at me and moved to the bed. It creaked as she sat. She patted the counterpane beside her.

"Won't you sit, Jed?"

To hear my name on her lips made me tremble with excitement. Conscious of the bulge in my pants, I stepped quickly over and sat down next to her.

"You're Charles White's boy, aren't you?"

I nodded, not sure if I could utter a sound. By God, she knew who I was! The sensation of her closeness was overwhelming. I could feel the warmth coming off her, like when you stand next to a horse in a stable in the wintertime.

"You came all the way to town just to see me?" She sounded surprised, but I was sure men would ride all the way from Mexico to see Pearl McCall. The whiskey and her proximity made me stupid. I couldn't concentrate on anything apart from trying to catch a better glimpse of her bosom.

She caught me looking, so I blurted out: "I haven't been able to think of anything else but you for coming on a month."

"That's sweet." She reached up and stroked my cheek. There was some soft fuzz growing on my top lip, but other than that, my face was smooth as an apple. "I remember now," she went on. "Your Pa was in Grafton's. It was a sunny day and you couldn't stop looking at me."

I had believed I'd hidden my desire for her, that my lust had been secret. It was humiliating to think she'd seen me gawping. I wondered if everyone else had known my feelings for Pearl. I was mortified. What I didn't understand then was that a lady, even one of the painted variety, wants to be noticed. That's why they primp, preen, brush their hair, and wear pretty dresses. There are few things a woman hates more than not being seen.

For a few seconds we sat in silence. A raucous braying laughter reached us from the saloon, disturbing the peaceful moment.

"Don't mind those boys," she said. "It's everyone's first time once. They're just jealous that yours is going to be with me." She laughed. It was a lovely sound, until she started to cough. For a time, she appeared incapable of stopping and the coughing seized hold of her, doubling her over. I didn't know what to do. I wanted to slap her on the back, like I would have done if Jacob or Beryl were coughing, but I could not bring myself to lay my hand upon Pearl, so I watched in dismay as she hacked and coughed for what seemed a long time.

She reached under the pillow for a handkerchief she kept there. She held it over her mouth. When the bout subsided, she waved a hand at a small dresser. There was a porcelain jug and a cup on it.

"Water, please," she whispered, not removing the handkerchief from her face.

I leapt up, glad to have been given something to do. Filling the cup, I carried it back to her. She drank a little. As she lowered the cup, I noticed a drop of blood on the rim. Quickly, she rubbed the porcelain clean, and dabbed at her lips.

"Sorry," she said.

A change had come over her. Gone was the confident woman of the saloon. She had been replaced by a timid, scared girl. Her slender form, beautiful as it was, now seemed frail. She appeared even more lovely to me in that moment, and I wanted nothing more than to hold her in my arms and fall onto the bed with her.

"Nothing to be sorry about," I said. "Can't help getting a cough."

She sighed, which brought on more coughing, though this time less violent.

"Would you be a darling and fetch the small bottle from the top drawer of the dresser?"

I snatched open the drawer and inside, on top of white undergarments, the sight of which made me all of a jitter, rested a tiny bottle of blue glass. I picked it up, delighting in the smooth touch of the cool linen and silks against my fingers. Blushing, sure she knew what I was thinking about, I handed her the bottle. I recognized it as laudanum. She poured a trickle into her cup of water, then drank the contents.

Seemingly revived from her coughing, she dabbed again at her lips, and passed the laudanum back to me.

"Could you put it back for me, please?" she said. Her cheeks were flushed, but her hands were icy as I took the bottle. I replaced it, this time taking a second to rub some of the soft fabrics between my fingers.

"Sorry," she said again. "The doctors said that the western air would do me good. But I'm getting no better." She handed me the empty cup and I placed it on the dresser. Our roles had somehow been reversed, and now it was her turn to be embarrassed, though what she had to be ashamed of, I didn't rightly know.

"What's wrong with you?" I asked, but I thought I already knew the answer.

"Consumption." Her voice was little more than a whisper.

Over the years I've heard many men saying lungers are the most beautiful of women. Whenever I hear that, I think back to that afternoon with Pearl. I'd had no idea she was sick until that moment, but perhaps that explained the perfection of her skin, like polished alabaster, and the shining, glistening of her eyes. They were deep and dark, like staring into a well at midnight.

Looking back with the eyes of an old man, I can see now that she was dying, but then, all I could take in was her fragile loveliness. Perhaps the beauty of the consumptive comes from their proximity to death. Whatever the truth of it, lunger or not, Pearl was the finest-looking woman I had ever seen.

The memory of her undergarments lingered on my fingers, and the heave of her bosom from all the coughing drew my gaze. I could not look away even if I had wanted to. Like a man seeing a mirage of water far in the distance in the Llano Estacado, I could not shake the sight from my mind.

I stood there in her room, looking down at her slim shape on the bed, and something changed in her eyes as she recognized my hunger. She surely noticed the tented cloth of my pants too, as my dick was still as stiff as a board.

Reaching behind her, she unfastened something and pulled her dress down to reveal her corset. I was entranced by the vision of her. Her plunging cleavage between the perfect, white breasts. I swallowed and licked my lips.

"Well," she said, in the manner of one resigned to hard labor, "we had better be getting on with it. I can't sit here yammering all day with you. Chewing the fat don't make me no money."

A cold hardness had entered her tone, and I felt as if she was disappointed in me. Sensing her displeasure, I felt disappointed in myself, though I couldn't rightly say why.

She pulled her bodice down to fully expose her pale bosom. I couldn't breathe now. Seeing my expression, she smiled, but there was no friendliness there.

"Come on," she said. "Time's a-wastin'. Not that you'll need more than a minute."

She hitched up her skirts, revealing her long, white legs. She wore nothing under her petticoats and when I saw the dark hair there, I thought I might faint. She lay back down on the bed and beckoned to me. I sensed the change in her, as clearly as if she had buckled on a gun belt, or painted her face for war as the Comanches did. With each movement, as she exposed more of her naked body, she brought back the previous confidence she had displayed, returning us to our original roles of whore and customer. Woman and boy.

Full of confusion at my conflicting emotions, I stepped timidly forward.

"You'll be needing to lose your pants, honey," she said, her voice sounding almost bored now.

This was a tune she had danced to many times before, and I felt as if I was under a spell. There was nothing I could do but follow her commands. I tugged at my belt and buttons. The moment my cotton pants fell around my ankles, she half rose and reached for my dick. The thrill of her touch made me gasp as if I'd stepped into a cold creek. She freed me from my drawers, then pulled me down onto her.

I had wondered about this moment hundreds of times, questioning if I would know what to do when the time came. Turns out I needn't have worried. There was nothing to it. And as soon as she pulled me inside her I stopped worrying about the change in her, her sickness, or whether I would do it right. In fact, I stopped thinking about pretty much everything.

SIX

It was over mighty quick. I shuddered with a warm sensation of delight after about a dozen increasingly frantic thrusts. Hell, I've seen bulls last longer and they do their business in seconds flat.

Pearl stroked my hair as I lay panting on top of her.

"There, there, sweet boy," she whispered. "That was nice, wasn't it?"

I forgot all about the change that had come over her before, and ignored that she still thought of me as a boy. She had called me sweet and I chose to believe she meant it. Perhaps, I thought, with my childish mind, we would be married. I could find some land and start my own ranch.

Before I could get as far as saying something truly stupid, she tapped me on the shoulder, indicating that I should get up. I rolled off and hastily yanked up my pants. Despite what we had just done, I did not want for her to see my scrawny nakedness.

I glanced down at her lying there, her hair splayed about her head. For a moment she lay still, her lips slightly parted in a half smile. I was so ecstatic, I was trembling. I felt like a hero in one of Jacob's dime paperbacks he sometimes let me read about knights in armor and damsels trapped in towers. I had ridden on this quest and I'd captured the heart of the lovely princess.

"You're a man now," she said, swinging her feet to the floor and pulling her clothes back into place. "You'll be wanting a whiskey to celebrate, I reckon." Her tone was abrupt, not exactly cruel, but to the point nonetheless, shattering my illusions that this was anything but a business transaction to her.

My stomach was sour from the whiskey, but at the mention of liquor, I realized she was right. I did want another slug to celebrate. I guess that was another first for that day: the moment the grog got a hold of me.

She was busying herself with remaking the bed, pulling the counterpane over the sheets, smoothing down the edges. The sunlight from the window accentuated her curves. I no longer had to imagine what her body was like beneath her skirts. And what I wanted more than anything in the world, was to have another taste.

She turned to face me, and, as if she had read my mind, she said: "You best be saving up your pennies and dimes if you'd like to see me again. Miss Alice don't let me work for free, even though for you, I would if I could." These words came as smooth and sickly as molasses. I'm sure she said similar to all her customers, but in that moment, I was certain we had something special between us.

"I'll be back as soon as I can," I said.

She guided me to the door.

"Don't take too long, Jed." Standing on her toes, she leaned in and kissed me on the cheek. "I'll be waiting." I felt like I might plumb-faint away.

She opened the door and gently pushed me out.

Stepping from her bright room into the shade of the saloon, I was left blinking on the landing. I was giddy. Pirooting with Pearl had got me all of a-glow and the whiskey had set my head spinning. I'd not eaten since that morning and the rotgut in my empty belly was doing its work. I'd been dizzy when I followed Pearl upstairs, now my vision began to swim and the world would not stay still.

"You gonna stand there all day, kid?"

The rough voice came from close by, making me jump. It was the tall cowboy from the bar, the one called Tom. He pushed himself away from the wall where he'd been leaning. He was smoking a cigarette. He took a draw and the coal glowed in the gloom. He stepped towards me, blowing smoke into my face.

I coughed, shaking my head to clear it. All I succeeded in doing was making myself dizzier.

"Get outta the way, kid," he drawled. "You've had your fun. And by God, you got your four dollars' worth. You've been in there longer than any of us were counting on. Did she have to help you find your pecker?"

He took another puff of his cigarette, then dropped it, crushing it beneath the toe of one of his shop-mades. He moved closer, forcing me to step aside.

I felt a flash of anger. He was treating me like a kid. I knew I shouldn't stand for it. A man would've lammed Tom, making him think twice about his insults. I clenched my fists, but made no move.

He stepped past me and the moment was gone. I watched in silent shame as he knocked gently on the door. It opened and there was Pearl, smiling in greeting.

"Tom," she said. "Come in, sugar."

"I've got my five dollars," he said with a chuckle. "I hope you're ready for a real man."

"I'm always ready for you," Pearl replied.

Looking back over his shoulder, Tom gave me a wink and followed her into the sunlit room that must have still smelt of me. Pearl ignored me, or perhaps she had not noticed me there behind Tom. Whatever the truth of it, she closed the door behind them, leaving me in the shadows.

A sudden gust of laughter came from the bar as if the men there had seen and heard my humiliation. I gritted my teeth, furious at myself for not standing up to Tom. Hurrying past the woman sitting at the top of the stairs, I stumbled down towards the bar.

SEVEN

"There he is." Gordon Sage waved at me from the Faro table. "You're a man now! Come and have another drink."

I heard the echo of Pearl's voice in his words. Tom's scorn was still fresh in my mind, and the timber boards beneath my feet seemed to buck and sway, as I imagine it must feel to a sailor on a stormy sea, though I have never once set foot on a ship. The thought of the burning taste of whiskey now made me feel sick. I wanted nothing less than to be the object of ridicule of the Triple Circle cowhands, so I headed for the swinging doors. The man who'd been groping Sally rose from his chair and I almost knocked him over.

"Easy there, kid," he growled.

I pushed past him.

"Hey, pard," Sage called after me, "what's the hurry?"

I ignored him.

It was bright and hot outside, but the gleam had come off the day, the way brass will tarnish if you don't polish it on the regular. I had a long ride back home ahead of me and I was suddenly concerned that I might not get there before nightfall. I'd told Ma that I wouldn't be back early, but I knew how she'd fret. She was likely to send Pa out to look for me if I wasn't home by sunset, no matter what I'd said. If that happened, I couldn't see how I would be able to maintain the lie I'd concocted about heading out to the high pasture, what with Collado Springs being in the opposite direction.

Buttermilk nodded his big head at the sight of me.

"Good to see you too," I whispered, stroking his velvety nose. "Hope you're ready for a run." He blew as if he understood my meaning, and I patted his neck. "Good. I'll be right back."

I walked quickly down the boardwalk towards the side of the saloon and the yard where I'd left Sam. I was doing my best not to replay the events from inside the saloon, but Godammit, that bastard Tom had spoilt the moment I'd had with Pearl.

I've never been able to explain it, call it intuition, but sometimes in my life I've known there was gonna be trouble before it struck me. That instinct has saved me on more than one occasion. That day, before I rounded the corner, through my anger at Tom and the whiskey that churned my guts and confused my thoughts, I suddenly knew something bad was about to go down. I told myself after that if I'd known how bad, I would have turned back. But I know now, that's a lie. I've never been one to turn away from trouble, and as I heard Sam's barking and a man's shouting, rather than slowing my pace, I increased it. I sped round the corner and into the yard at a lope.

The yard was pretty much as I'd left it, except that the wagon was now empty and a great pile of barrels, sacks and crates stood by the side door of the saloon. The mules were still hitched, their sweat drying on their flanks. The shirtless negro was motionless. His dark skin was glistening from his exertions, and bright red blood streamed from his nose. He raised his eyes to glare at me, but he seemed to pay no heed to his bleeding.

Sam was where I had tied him, but instead of lying patiently for my return, he was snarling and growling. As I watched, the old teamster, who loomed over Sam, whipped him with a rawhide quirt. Sam yelped, then strained at the cord I had tied him with, snapping his jaws at the bearded man. He stepped back quickly out of range of the dog's teeth, with more agility than I would have expected for a man of his years.

"Try to bite me, would ya, cur?" he spat, taking another swing with the rawhide. It connected with Sam's snout, making him yowl.

"Stop it!" I shouted.

He turned a bloodshot stare at me and I could see he was drunk, and mean, the way only a drunk can be.

"Your dog needs to be learnt manners," he slurred. Stepping close again without warning, he swung the quirt, landing a vicious, stinging blow against Sam's back.

"Stop it!" I shouted again. Even as I spoke, I knew he would not listen to me. Ignoring me, he hit Sam again.

Without thinking, I rushed at him, taking advantage of the fact he had dismissed me as a boy who could cause him no harm. I was not yet fully growed, still a skinny youth, but I was wiry and strong from working the land. And I was angry, and not a little drunk myself.

I shoved him hard and he staggered back several paces, colliding with the nearest of his mules. The animal shook its head and brayed. Struggling to keep my balance, now that the whiskey had taken a hold of me, I bent down to untie Sam. But before I could release him, the teamster bellowed and charged at me.

"Looks like I need to learn you some manners too," he roared.

Jacob and I often fought each other, so I'd been in my share of fist fights, but I had never before stood toe-to-toe with a grown man. Much as I had wanted to fool myself, I was still a boy. I tried to meet his attack head on, but he was as solid as an old oak stump, and despite being drunk, years of hard work had made him strong. He clattered into me, brushing aside my swinging punches and dishing out a couple fast jabs to my face.

His blows rocked me back on my heels. He had space now and landed a boot straight between my legs. I collapsed immediately, thinking I might puke from the agony. I've heard women say there is no worse pain than childbirth, but that is only because they don't have balls that have been given a good kick. I've been beaten, stabbed, burnt and shot, and I'd take any of those every day of the week and twice on Sundays over being punted in the cojones.

Seeing he'd knocked the sand out of me, he turned back to his previous task. Sam had not stopped barking, and now Woodrow retrieved his quirt from where he had dropped it and laid into him, striking the poor dog over and over.

People talk about seeing red, but in my experience it is more like seeing black. I was already furious at Tom's comments, and seeing the teamster's treatment of my dog had further enraged me. Now the agony from Woodrow's kick radiated out from my groin and seemed to burn away any rational thought, replacing it with whiskey-fueled rage. I surged to my feet, my vision darkening as if I was looking through smoke.

"I'm gonna kill you," I hissed.

My words must have cut through to Woodrow because he turned to me, pausing in his punishment of my dog.

"How're you gonna do that, boy?" he sneered, his voice dripping with sarcasm. He glanced down at my hips. "You ain't even packing iron."

"I don't need no smoke wagon to kill a coward like you," I said, hearing the words I spoke as if from a distance.

He looked at me with disdain, shaking his head, half amused that I should be so bold.

But I was not lying. I had helped Pa and Jacob often enough slaughtering the hogs to know how it was done. The only difference was that this pig wore clothes and walked on two legs.

Leaping forward, I pulled my knife from my belt. At the last moment, Woodrow's eyes widened. Perhaps he recognized in me what so many have seen since. Larry Woodrow was a mean drunk, but there is none meaner than Jedediah White, and as I sprang at him, he saw the mortal danger he was in.

He tried to step back, raising his hands to ward off my attack. But it was too late for him. Grabbing hold of his right hand in my left, I plunged the knife into his belly. He grunted as the steel went in. I tugged it out and his blood was warm on my hand. His eyes widened still further as he understood what had happened.

"You son of a bitch," he wheezed, his voice rising in pitch and volume. His strong hands clawed at me.

But he was no match for me now. I had seemed to gain strength with my fury and hurt, and my head was filled with blackness as I stabbed him again and again.

Sam didn't stop barking until Larry Woodrow was dead.

EIGHT

A sudden chill came over me as I stared down at the teamster's corpse. I'd never killed a man before. I felt no remorse for what I had done. He had it coming. But I knew what happened to murderers in the territory. If people didn't throw a neck-tie sociable right there and then, killers would wait for the district judge to come to Collado Springs to pass verdict. The outcome would be the same, the only difference being that the rope would be connected to a scaffold instead of slung over the branch of an old oak. In many ways I was still only a boy, but if that day had shown me anything it was that I was old enough to gamble, drink, fuck, and now, kill. I was pretty sure the new state of Texas would think me old enough to swing for my crimes too.

I started to weep.

I'm not proud to say it, but at the thought of dying I began to blubber like a baby. I didn't think about the shame that I would bring on my Ma and Pa, or even of the life I had taken against the Lord's Commandments. I thought of myself, and that I would never get to do all the things I'd imagined my life would bring. A few months before, I'd gone through a spell of worrying I might die a virgin. Now that wasn't going to happen, I sniveled to think I would never get to dip my pecker again.

The one time with Pearl had been over much too soon and I wasn't sure I had done it right. Like a man who is thrown from his horse trying to jump a ditch, I wanted nothing more than to take another run at that gully.

A shadow fell over me, bringing me back to the present. I spun around, brandishing the bloody knife. I'd killed once and for a second, I wondered if I was going to need to kill again to keep from being brought to justice.

It was the negro, Hannibal. He loomed over me, making me feel small and insignificant. Where I was hunched over, my slender shoulders shaking, tears streaking my dirty face, snot dribbling from my nose, he was still and solid. The great slabs of his chest shone with sweat; the muscles of his arms bulged. I glanced at his hands, terrified he might have a weapon, though in all honesty, even armed as I was, I don't believe he would have needed more than his fists to beat me. Even so, I raised my knife menacingly.

"No time for that," he said, his voice surprisingly calm. I realized I had not heard him speak before this instant. His was a deep resonant voice and it fit him perfectly, the tone as powerful and strong as his physique.

I backed away, fearing he meant to avenge his master. He lashed out, catching my wrist in his huge callused grip and squeezing hard.

I yelped and let go of the knife. It landed on Woodrow's belly with a squelching slapping sound. The numerous stab wounds were still oozing blood and his shirt was sodden.

"I said there's no time for that," he repeated.

I cowered, imagining he planned to hit me. Instead, he let me go.

"No time for crying neither," he said. "Pick up your knife." I stared at him, eyes wide. I could not speak. "Do you want to be found here?" he hissed. "Like this?" He looked down at his master's dead body. "Even a white boy like you would find it difficult to explain this."

His voice was still level, giving the semblance of calm, but I could see the flicker of panic building up in his eyes.

As if awakening from a dream, I looked about the yard. There were the barrels, sacks and crates. The wagon had not moved and was still hitched to the sad-looking mules. Sam had stopped barking, but now whimpered as if he understood that I had done something terrible. I swayed on my feet, dizzy and barely believing. I seemed incapable of motion.

Hannibal snatched up my knife. I flinched, but he held it out to me handle first.

"Take it and put it away," he said. An edge of tension colored his voice now, like the purple tinge on the horizon before a gully washer rolls down from the Guadalupe Mountains. "Then help me with this evil-hearted bastard."

Seeing that he did not mean me harm, I took the knife. It was covered in congealing blood, but there was no time to clean it now. He was right, there was no time for weeping and self-pity either. The longer we stood there, the more likely we would be discovered. Ignoring the blood that covered my hands, I shoved the knife into the sheath on my belt.

Hannibal had taken a hold of Woodrow's hands and half lifted him from the dusty ground that was now dark with blood. The bearded face lolled. Thankfully the man's open eyes were not looking at me. I didn't move. Shaking my head, I wondered if I might puke on the teamster's dead body. The thought made my stomach clench and I swallowed back bile.

"Don't just stand there staring," said Hannibal, his deep voice growing increasingly anxious. "Help me get him into the wagon. Nobody's seen us, but that won't last long."

It was true. Unbelievably there was no shouting from outraged witnesses to my crime and the noise from the busy street continued unabated. Far off, down near Grafton's perhaps, a voice was raised in song and someone started to play the fiddle.

"Come on!" Hannibal said.

I stooped and took hold of Woodrow's boots. He was heavy, but Hannibal was strong and with my help we soon had him in the wagon bed and covered with a tarp. Miraculously, still nobody seemed to have seen us and Collado Springs went about its business without interruption.

"I'll turn the rig around," said Hannibal. "Go get your horse. You can tie it to the wagon."

"I ain't going with you," I said, confused. All I wanted was to run.

He shook his head and began to cajole the mules into motion.

"Yes, you are," he rumbled. "You got me into this. You need to help me out of it. And don't you dare think about running."

When I look back, I wonder if my memory serves me well or if I have chosen to remember Hannibal issuing commands to me as if he were my superior. I know nothing of who he had been before I met him, but just minutes before he had been enslaved and appeared to obey his master without dissent. Though to judge from the scars on his back, perhaps he had not always been the most biddable of slaves.

Whatever the truth, I recall Hannibal telling me what to do, and I chose to do it. I think I was content to have someone take charge, and it did not strike me as strange then that the man to do so happened to be a negro slave. My mind was reeling from what I had done, and it has often been my experience that in a moment of stress, people are pleased to follow the lead of anyone who speaks clearly and with conviction.

I hurried to the hitching rail out front of the saloon. A group of women and children were walking along the other side of the street and I was frightened that they were staring at me. Surely they had seen the blood on my hands and must have known what I had done.

"Hey, Jed! There you are."

The voice, close by, almost made my heart stop. Gordon Sage and a couple of the cowhands from the Triple Circle had come out onto the boardwalk and were stood smoking and leaning on the rail, watching the day go by. Sage's eyes followed the women in their bright dresses across the street, even as he spoke to me.

"You ready for that whiskey now?"

I hesitated, unsure of the best course of action. Perhaps if I went with Sage, I could be done with Hannibal and the grisly secret in the back of the wagon. But Sam was still tied in the yard, and I could not leave him. Besides, if I did not return, no matter how unlikely, perhaps Hannibal would give me away as Woodrow's killer. But before I'd had time to process all of these thoughts and to formulate an answer, the need for a reply was taken away from me.

The cow puncher next to Sage, pointed down the street and nudged his friend.

"We got trouble," he said, sounding excited by the prospect.

Sage and I both looked. Staggering up the center of the street, people scattering before him, came Slim Denby. Somewhere along the way, he'd lost his hat and he was squinting in the bright sun, the light gleaming off his balding head. In his hands he brandished a double-barreled fowling piece.

"Sage!" Slim shouted. I couldn't be sure if he'd seen the object of his anger on the boardwalk, but he kept walking determinedly towards Brent's. "I'm coming for you, you yellow-bellied son of a bitch, and you better be heeled this time."

The shout drew the attention of the women across the street. Catching sight of the gun-toting cowpoke, one of them screamed and they all hurried into a boarding house for safety.

"Shit," said Sage. "Looks like that whiskey will have to wait, Jed."

I didn't reply. Seizing the moment of distraction, I rushed to Buttermilk, unlooped his reins, and pulled him towards the side of Brent's and the yard beyond.

Sam greeted me as I rounded the corner, barking and gamboling. Hannibal must have freed him from his tether. Buttermilk snorted and shook his mane at the hound's antics, but he was not frightened. He was used to Sam.

The wagon had been turned around and Hannibal was already up on the driver's seat.

"Tie your horse to the cart and come on up here beside me."

For a second, I felt a stab of anger at being bossed about by a negro, but then I nodded and did what I was told. It was easier than having to think about what I had done and what came next.

Hannibal shook the reins and clicked his tongue. The mules heaved against their collars, knocking and rattling the traces. They were tired, but the wagon was empty now, apart from the two of us and Woodrow's corpse, so it didn't take them much effort to get us going. Creaking and groaning, the wagon trundled out into the sunlit street.

I glanced down at the ground where Woodrow had fallen. The dirt was stained dark and I tried to imagine it as someone else might see it. Was it obvious it was blood that had colored the dust?

"Head north," I said. That would take me further from home, but people's attention was focused in the other direction where Slim was standing in the dusty road, still shouting. Gordon Sage was nowhere to be seen. He must have slipped back into the saloon.

Hannibal said nothing, but he turned the wagon to the north and in a few minutes, we were passing the tents on the edge of the city limits.

NINE

We rode in silence until we could no longer see the shapes of Collado Spring's buildings behind us. Soon after we left the town, when we'd covered perhaps half a mile, we heard shots echo across the flat land. Neither of us spoke, each lost in our thoughts. I wondered if Sage had gunned down Slim. It seemed to me that the drunk had been asking for it all day. But perhaps it was Sage who was buzzard food. I wondered if he was slick with a gun. I'd always wanted to see a real gunhand in action. Whatever had happened, it would surely keep the sheriff and his deputies busy for a while, which would give us more time.

Time for what?

We were headed in the opposite direction from my home and there was no way I'd be back before sunset now. I wanted to jump down from the wagon, climb onto Buttermilk and ride away as fast as I could, hoping the law would never find me.

I don't know what Hannibal was thinking, but as we traveled along the rutted road that led straight as a buffalo spear towards the mountains rising in the hazy distance, his whole demeanor changed. His shoulders sagged and he stared at the backs of the mules as if they would give him an answer to his problems.

My racing heart had slowed, but its pounding must have

burnt up most of the whiskey, because my head was clearing now. Gone was the panicky feeling that we would be caught at any moment. Now I could imagine we might find a way out of this mess. I replayed the moment when I had stabbed Woodrow over in my mind, but no matter how many times I thought about it, I could summon no remorse. I used to wonder if there was something wrong with my head, but I gave up trying to figure that out years ago. You only have the brains you were born with and you have to make do with what you got. I've been described as cold and calculating, and that is no doubt true. But such traits have served me well over the years, and the men I served with during the War Between the States certainly never had reason to complain about me when it came to facing the enemy. It is a fact that many men freeze up when presented with a difficult situation and danger to their person. I do not. Once I have made a decision, I act on it and move on. I've always been like that, and back then in that jouncing and rattling wagon, I had pushed aside any qualms I might have had about what I had done and thought only of the future.

"I think we made it," I said, breaking the silence that had settled between us.

Hannibal let out a long sigh, then turned to look at me. His eyes were red, as if he had been crying, though I knew he had not.

"You made it," he said, his tone flat.

"We're both here, ain't we?" I swept a hand around us, indicating there was no other person in sight. "We got out of town. Nobody saw us."

He shook his head, but said nothing. I'd been thinking and had come up with a plan of sorts. Granted, it wasn't much of a plan, but it was all I could think of. I'd been happy to do as Hannibal said for a time, but he appeared to have lost his nerve, so now I needed to take control.

"There's a gulch down that aways," I pointed off to the west. "If we leave his body down there, the coyotes will get to him. With any luck nobody will find him for days. Or even weeks. If they do, he'll be so ate up nobody will recognize him."

Hannibal was glowering into the distance now, his jaw set, muscled bulging.

"You can be free," I said.

He snapped his head around to stare at me. His eyes were wide, incredulous of my ignorance of the world.

His world.

"Free?" For the first time, he raised his voice and I thought he might strike me. "Free?" he repeated, almost choking on the word.

"Isn't that what you want?" I asked.

He laughed then, and there was no humor in that sound. It is hard to fill laughter with sorrow, but somehow Hannibal managed it.

"You're as mean as old master Woodrow back there," he said at last.

"I didn't mean you no harm," I said.

"You didn't mean... you didn't mean for anything to happen, I guess. White boy who never wanted for nothing in his life. But you didn't mean it, so it's all good, ain't that right?"

I shook my head.

"Don't you want to be free?"

"Of course I wanna be free, boy," he spat. "You think I be free now?"

"Woodrow is dead."

"Yeah, that's right. This morning I had a master who whipped me and cussed me all day long. I know what you thought of him. I could see the way you looked at him. The pity in your eyes when you looked at me. You think I ain't seen pity from rich little white folks before?"

"He treated you worse than his mules," I whispered.

"He did that. And now he's dead. So I have no master. But how does that make me free?"

I said nothing.

"Look at me!" he went on, his fury spilling out. "You think I can just ride off and start a new life? You think nobody will ask me where I come from? How I came to be on my own?" He took a deep breath, but I knew he was not done. "And did you think I might have a wife? Children?" His voice trembled. "What am I supposed to do with them now? I can't just ride back like nothing happened. You never stopped to think about me, did ya?" He was breathing hard now. His hands gripped the reins so tight I thought he might snap the leather. "And don't be telling me you killed the old bastard to free my poor black self from the bonds of slavery. It had nothing to do with me. I saw your eyes when he hit your dog. You killed him 'cause he whipped your animal. He only did it 'cause your dog tried to stop him striking me. That hound has more heart than you." He said nothing for a while. I was silent, disbelieving of the rage he had directed at me. Sam loped along beside the cart, tongue lolling. He'd be content to run beside me forever, I reckoned. "I figure that says something good about you at least," Hannibal said at last. "You care about that mutt and he seems to care about you."

I didn't know what to say. He was right. About all of it. Larry Woodrow had been mean to his animals and to his slave. He probably thought of them in the same way: as beasts of burden, to do his bidding, and for him to abuse as he saw fit. Was I really any different? I had been angry when I saw how the teamster had neglected his mules. I hadn't liked the story told by the scars on Hannibal's back, but it hadn't been till Woodrow'd hit Sam that I'd seen black.

"Head off the road here," I said, pointing into the west. I figured nothing I said could change things or make things right for Hannibal, so I said nothing more on the subject.

Hannibal didn't answer, but a second later, he pulled on the reins and the mules stoically hauled us, bumping and rocking, off the road.

TEN

We trailed off the road for a spell until we came to the gulch I'd mentioned. It was just a draw, with a few cottonwood trees clinging to the crumbling edges of the gully. There was no water in the bottom then, but when storms rolled in, it would turn into a torrent.

Hannibal and I didn't talk much more. It seemed we had said all there was to say. Nothing would change what I'd done or the decisions we'd made to get there. I didn't ask him what he planned to do. I didn't want to know. He was right. I hadn't thought of him at all and I didn't want to be reminded of my guilt in that regard.

We unhitched the mules and they stood in the hot afternoon, heads down. I had thought about killing one of the animals, to make things look more believable, but when the time came, the dumb beast staring at me with its forlorn eye, I could not bring myself to do it. I have never had a problem with killing men who deserve it, but I can't abide harming a defenseless animal, unless it's for eating. If Hannibal decided to eat one of the mules, that was his concern and he could do the butchering.

"Take 'em both," I said, and Hannibal shrugged.

He clambered into the wagon and came back with a leather

bag he had taken from Woodrow. He tipped the contents onto the driver's seat. There was a small folding knife, a pouch of tobacco, a box of lucifers and a purse that jingled with hard money. Also inside the bag was a Colt Walker pistol, along with a powder flask, and a pouch of percussion caps and balls. I was interested in the chink, of which there was just over forty dollars, but the gun drew my eye most of all. I picked it up, marveling at the heft of the thing. It was a brute of a gun, weighing close to five pounds unloaded. But it felt instantly right in my hand.

Hannibal counted out the money into two piles. He was fast at it and I wondered at his story, and if all slaves were so well-versed in numbers. He handed me half the money and I pocketed it without a word. He made no mention of the gun, and I made no offer of it. I could not imagine parting with it. Nor did I once consider letting him keep more than half the money. I knew he would have more need of cash, but I wanted to visit Pearl again, and the twenty dollars made me rich.

I stuck the pistol in my saddle bags and moved to the back of the wagon, keen to be done and far away from the place. The stink of the dead man was strong now. He had soiled himself as the dead do and the air inside the covered wagon bed was hot and fetid. Once more, Hannibal climbed into the wagon. He manhandled Woodrow's stiffening body onto the driver's seat.

Hannibal did not speak as he released the brake, dropped down to the ground and made his way to the rear of the vehicle. We were silent as we put our shoulders to the wagon. For a moment I thought it wouldn't budge and we'd have to hitch one of the mules again after all. But Hannibal grunted and the wagon started to roll, slowly at first, then faster as it reached the slope at the lip of the gully. In seconds, it was moving too fast for us to keep up with and we watched, breathing hard and sweating, as it toppled into the small ravine, snapping saplings and brush, until it stopped with a splintering crash, resting on its side against the trunk of an old cottonwood. Woodrow had been thrown out of the wagon and I could see his boots and the top of his dirty pants jutting from underneath one of the front wheels.

Nobody would see the wagon or Woodrow unless they rode within a hundred yards of the gulch. It was still open range back then, and at that time of year, it could be weeks before anyone stumbled on the scene of the 'accident'.

I swung myself up onto Buttermilk. He skittered and I had to hold his reins tight to prevent him from running off. He had been tied behind the wagon and the stench of the corpse must have been driving him crazy. Besides, he was young and strong and had not been carrying me for some time, so he was ready to head for home at a lope.

"Good luck," I said.

Hannibal was preparing a makeshift saddle for one of the mules out of a blanket and some of the harness.

"Don't think I know what good luck is," he said, without looking at me.

I was suddenly filled with the dread that he would be caught. That he would point the finger at me.

As if he could sense my thoughts, he said, "Don't you worry yourself over me, little master. I ain't going to tell nobody what happened."

I hesitated. He looked up at me sitting on my horse.

"You gonna have to trust me on that," he said. "Or you wanna kill me too?"

The thought flashed through my mind. He was much stronger than me, but I had a gun now. Not that I knew how to use it. Besides, he'd done nothing to me. I had thrown his life into disarray. He was just making the best of the cards he'd been dealt.

"I ain't gonna kill you," I said.

He chuckled his sad laughter, as if I'd told a joke.

"No, you ain't," he said. Still laughing quietly, he went back to fixing his saddle.

"Good luck," I repeated, and pulled Buttermilk's nose to the south. I gave him his head and we were soon speeding over the plain, Sam running along beside us. I looked over my shoulder and after only a short while I couldn't see Hannibal no more.

Despite his promise, as I rode home, I couldn't shake the feeling that he would be caught and would give me away to save his hide. Still, there was nothing I could do about it. I pushed my worries aside and headed for the ranch.

ELEVEN

Three days went by and I began to think I'd gotten away with killing Larry Woodrow. But on the fourth morning after I'd come back from my clandestine trip to Collado Springs, a group of riders approached the house from the south. It was a hot day. The sky was the pure blue of a starling's egg and the only clouds to be seen were wisps high over the distant mountains. For the first time since I'd arrived home, I felt that stab of fear I'd encountered as we'd carried Woodrow's bloody body to the wagon, and driven out of town.

It was the pang of worry that I would be found out. My neck began to itch as I imagined the rawhide noose tightening about my throat.

Shielding my eyes, I peered across the hazed scrubby land at the riders, trying to make them out. There were four of them, and they came slowly, with no sign of haste. I took a deep breath, forcing myself to be calm. It was not uncommon for riders to come to the house. Other ranchers or travelers would stop and ask for a meal or a cup of coffee. Cowhands riding the grub line sometimes rolled in too, especially when the weather was bad. Ma liked to hear news of the wider world and was always happy to feed such guests. If it was late, Pa would let them bunk with the vaqueros.

They came from the same direction I had ridden in from three nights prior, after leaving Hannibal far off to the north. The moon had been up and it was after midnight when I'd arrived. I had been prepared for Ma's worry, so, even though it took me an extra hour of riding, I'd circled our land to approach the house from the direction of the high pasture. I knew I was going to be grilled with questions, the last thing I needed was to give Ma and Pa reason to think I was being deceitful.

As it was, they did not suspect anything more than that I had lost track of time, as I had done on other occasions. I could tell that Ma had thought something terrible had befallen me. She had been keeping a tight rein on her emotions, making coffee and even sewing a while by the light of a lamp, but when I rode up out of the night, she had been unable to contain her tears. She embraced me tightly, all the while scolding me for being so late.

"I told you I might be late, Ma," I said. "Heck, I thought about setting up camp down by the creek and riding in for breakfast."

"You should have done," Pa said, his voice gruff. "You're no Indian. Riding in the dark is a fool's errand. You're lucky Buttermilk didn't step in a gopher hole and snap his leg."

"Oh, Charles," Ma exclaimed, gripping his arm, "don't say such things. Now I won't be able to think of anything else if the boys are out after sundown."

"Then they had best not be out after sundown," growled Pa. He didn't say as much, but I could tell he had been worried too.

"Don't fret, Ma," I said, accepting the cup of coffee she handed me. "I'm careful."

"How were the head up there?" Pa asked, following behind us as we went inside. The house was filled with the smell of pork and beans that Ma had left warming for me on the stove.

"One of the calf's had fallen into a gulch. Took me a while to rope him and haul him out. He managed to get hisself cut up some on some broken mesquite, but he'll live."

I'd thought of the story as I was riding home. I needed

something to explain the blood on my shirt and pants. I'd stopped at the creek and washed my knife and hands as well as I could, but there was no hiding that something, or someone, had bled on my clothes.

Pa snorted and I wondered if he suspected anything untoward.

"If the wolves and coyotes don't take him," he said, frowning.

"There are a lot of new head all over those ridges," I said. "A passel with no brands. Should we bring them down for branding?"

"Happen we should," Pa said. He seemed pleased that for once I had anticipated a chore. I was not a natural rancher and I didn't often apply myself to the workings of the spread unless I was told to. "Why'd you decide to ride up there anyhow?" he asked.

"Sometimes I just like to ride and think," I said, taking a spoonful of pork and beans. "Thought if I was gonna to be on my own for the day, I'd make myself useful."

Ma and Pa exchanged a look and I wondered if I was pushing it too far. Perhaps they thought I was growing up. They had no idea how much growing I had done that day.

On that first night, I couldn't sleep. I was tuckered out, but my mind wouldn't slow down. I recalled how Woodrow's blood had been hot on my hand. I remembered the sour smell of his dying breath. I could hardly believe it had been so easy to kill him, and me just a kid with a knife.

As soon as he saw me the next morning, Jacob had known something had happened. Over breakfast Pa said that we would have to round up the cattle that was dispersed over the high pasture and made me tell my story again. I could see that Jacob wanted to call me out for my lies, but he caught my eye and said nothing. We had learnt that it was better for both of us to keep our secrets between us brothers. He had expected me to spill the beans when we were alone fixing the corral in the blistering dusty heat of the afternoon. We usually told each other everything, but no matter how he pried, I stuck to my guns. I had ridden up to check on the stock, I said, nothing more.

He got angry after a while, and left me to complete the job on my own. But I had decided I couldn't tell him what had happened. Not then, perhaps not ever.

As the days went by I began to think I had gotten away with it. I'd wrapped the Colt and ammunition in my slicker and hidden it along with the money under a rock out by an old hackberry tree. That had been the first secret I'd kept from Jacob, and I wondered absently if keeping secrets was another thing that happened when you grew up and became a man.

Since my return, I walked tall around the place with more of a swagger. On a couple of occasions, I caught Ma watching me from the stoop. I figured she was thinking how her little boy had grown up all of a sudden. Truth was, I felt like things had changed. I was filled with a new-found confidence, partly from having at long last greased my axle with Pearl, but if I am truly honest, it was the killing of Larry Woodrow that had really made the difference. I had taken a man's life and I had been shocked at how easy a task that had been. It seemed to me that nothing bad had come from the act. I told myself that I'd freed Hannibal, and I'd come out of the whole affair richer by twenty dollars.

All my swagger vanished and my balls shriveled like dried chilies when Jacob, who had the eyes of a hawk, called out from the other side of the barn where he was watching the four riders coming across our land.

"It's Sheriff Bourland," he called out. Seeing the sheriff out this far from town was usually cause for excitement, as he would bring news of the latest happenings in the county. But on that day, I could imagine only one thing that brought him to our door. Sweat trickled down the back of my neck. Fighting to remain calm, I climbed over the corral fence and sauntered over towards the house, not rushing at all.

"Good afternoon, Sheriff," Ma was saying as I arrived. "Would you care for a cup of coffee. And I have some biscuits if you're hungry. There's not enough for more than one each, but you are very welcome to what there is."

"Just the coffee would be fine, Eliza," he said, swinging down from his large paint horse.

"I wouldn't say no to a biscuit," said a younger man who wore a deputy's badge.

"You'd never say no to any food," said Bourland. "Don't worry about feeding us," he went on to Ma, shaking his head.

"It's no trouble at all," she replied and hurried inside.

Bourland gave the deputy a hard look as the men all dismounted.

"Don't you ever think of anything but your belly?" he asked. The deputy didn't reply, but had the decency to look abashed.

"He thinks about other things as well," said a dark-skinned man in a dusty black suit. If his complexion didn't do the job, his accent made it clear he was from west of the Pecos. "Just ask Pearl at old Brent's. I hear Ernest's her favorite customer. He's hungry all the time because he spends all his dinero on whores."

"Why you greaser son of a bitch," the young deputy snarled.

The mention of Pearl got under my skin and I glared at him.

"Now, boys, watch your mouths," the sheriff said. "There's a lady and young 'uns here." He nodded towards me and the fact that he saw me as a child made me even angrier. But his eyes did not linger on me. In fact, he seemed to ignore me, returning his gaze to Ma, as she stepped out of the house with a plate of biscuits.

Perhaps I was not about to be unveiled as a killer after all. I stepped up onto the porch. Jacob was close behind me.

"What's got you riding over this way?" he asked, assuming the role of the man of the house in my father's absence.

"Well, howdy, Jacob," said the sheriff around a mouthful of biscuit. "Your Pa not around?"

"He's ridden over yonder with a couple of the vaqueros," Jacob pointed to the east.

"I wanted to talk with your Pa." Bourland finished his biscuit and wiped his moustache with the back of his fingers. For a while he stared off at the horizon, perhaps weighing up what to say next. Mind made up, he looked back at Jacob and

Ma. Again, he ignored me, which I could only think was a good sign. Even so, it rankled. I have ever been a proud man and often it has led me into problems. "I don't suppose there is any harm speaking to you," he said.

"What is it, sheriff?" Ma asked, her voice quivering with anxiety. "You look like you've been in the saddle a while."

"We slept rough last night. Truth is we ain't ridden too far."

"Too far for me," said the fourth man, rubbing his behind. He was a squat fellow with a small hat that would be no good for keeping the sun off. The others said nothing, but from their exchanged looks it was clear this was not the first time he'd complained. The Mexican spat off the porch into the dust.

"It's been a busy couple days, that's for sure," said Bourland, ignoring the small man. He held out his cup for some more coffee and Ma obliged. Her eyes glimmered and I noticed how all the men watched her movements. Their attention made me uncomfortable.

"Has there been trouble in town?" Jacob asked, keen to be part of proceedings.

"There sure has. It was pay day for the Triple Circle, end of last week. That's always a vexatious time, what with all the cowhands in off the ranch."

"We heard about that poor piano player," said Ma. "And the no firearms regulation. I was saying to Charles just the other day that it was a good idea. No civilized men have need of firearms in town."

Sheriff smiled.

"My thinking exactly. It has helped somewhat, but trouble is you can't confiscate all the guns. And certainly not from the least civilized."

"Someone was shot?" I asked, unable to keep quiet. Ever since hearing the gunfire ring out as Hannibal and I rode away, I had wondered what had happened.

Bourland turned to look at me.

"Unfortunately, not just one someone," he said. He sipped his coffee.

"What happened?" asked Jacob, desperate not to be left out

of the conversation.

"Two cow punchers went at it." Bourland lifted his hat and scratched at his greasy hair. "One with a scattergun, the other with a pistol. They had both deposited their own guns at my office, so I have no idea where they got the weapons. Nobody's owning up to it now."

"They died?" I asked.

"One of them took the big jump right there and then. Man by the name of Slim Denby. Got drilled straight through the heart."

I let out my breath, only then realizing I'd been holding it. I liked Gordon Sage and didn't like the idea of him being killed, especially not by a dunderhead like Slim Denby.

"Who was the other guy?" asked Jacob. "Was he slick with his pistol? He must have been to shoot him in the heart."

Sheriff Bourland sighed.

"He was slick enough," he said. "But not fast enough to dodge a barrel of buckshot." He shook his head. "Slim let him have it with his dying breath. He was so drunk that even as close as he was, he almost missed him. If he'd hit him square on Sage Gordon would be lying alongside him in the bone orchard. As it is, he took the best part of a cartridge in the face. He's lucky to be alive, but he ain't gonna win no beauty contests."

"Lucky to have kept one eye too," said the short man. Everybody ignored him. The Mexican spat into the yard again.

"He lost an eye?" I asked, imagining the handsome cowhand who had joshed with me and bought me whiskey. I learnt a couple of important lesson right then: don't stand in front of a man with a loaded gun if you can help it, especially not a scatter gun that he barely needs to aim. And if you mean to kill a man, don't allow him to get his shot off.

"That he did," Bourland replied, his tone somber. "With any luck, he'll recover. Might even be able to work again, though it is never easy to predict what might happen to a man after such an injury."

The others all looked at their feet and nodded grimly.

I wondered what it would do to a man such as Sage, to be

disfigured and then perhaps not be able to do the things he had excelled at. Would he be able to ride and rope again?

"You hear that, boys?" Ma said, her face pale. "That's why I don't want you going into town. It's much too dangerous. You're safer out here on the ranch."

"About that," said the sheriff. "Have you noticed any strangers on your land in the last few days?"

"Indians?" Ma asked, sounding terrified at the prospect. The thought of an attack by Comanches was a constant worry, but the fact of it was they had been pushed into Indian Territory and it was too risky for them to come hunting scalps so close to civilization.

"No, no, nothing like that," said Bourland. "Probably just one man. Maybe a negro, riding a stolen horse."

"Could be a white, or a Mexican," said the small man. Nobody paid him any mind.

"The sign we was following weren't from no Indian," said the Mexican.

"You don't know who you are following?" I asked.

"Truth is we don't, son," said Bourland. It's the damnedest thing. Pardon my language, ma'am." He pulled the brim of his hat. "Couple nights ago, I got called out to McCulloch's place. Some of his hands had come across a negro on their land. A big fella, skin as black as midnight. He didn't seem used to riding the range. He'd built a fire that could be seen for miles. Such a waste of timber for just one man. It ain't even cold."

"Stupid too," said the Mexican. "For a man on the run."

Bourland nodded.

"If there's one thing I've learnt in my years as a lawman, it's that there's a lot more stupid people out there than you'd like to think. In his case, I guess it is in his kind's nature." He shrugged, deciding not to proceed with his thoughts on the mind of the negro. "He had been riding a mule and leading another," he continued. "McCulloch's hands asked him where he was coming from and where he was headed, but the boy was tight-lipped. They could see he had stolen the mules and that like as not he had run away from his master." Bourland sniffed and shook his head. "Turns out he'd done worse than that. A couple of the cow punchers followed his back trail a ways and found a wagon in the bottom of a gully. Underneath it was a teamster. He was known to them."

"Who was it?" I asked.

"A man by the name of Larry Woodrow. He visited town every month or two."

I kept my face blank of recognition. Ma looked at me and Sheriff Bourland held my gaze for a few seconds before continuing.

"This Woodrow had been killed, stabbed many times. That's why McCulloch sent for me. It was my intention to question the negro about what had happened, but it seems that some of McCulloch's boys couldn't wait for me to arrive and decided to question him themselves." He sighed, and took another mouthful of his coffee. "He was beat up real bad when I got there. By some kind of miracle, he was still alive. Almost felt like he'd fought to keep breathing for me." He snorted at the idea. "Who knows what goes on in such a man's head? Perhaps he wished to unburden his black soul. Whatever the reason, when he saw me, he pulled me close and told me everything."

"Everything?" I asked, unable to keep quiet.

"He told me how he had stabbed the teamster to death, and then positioned the wagon to look like an accident, hoping the wild animals would dispose of the evidence of his crime."

"Did you hang him?" Jacob asked, sounding hopeful.

The sheriff shook his head.

"No need. He died shortly after."

I thought of Hannibal and his sorrowful laugh. Did he have a wife and children as he had implied? The sweat on my back was cold, despite the heat of the day. I shuddered. I'd done this. Just as surely as if I'd buried the knife into him too. My actions had killed another man, and this one had done nothing to warrant death. His only crime that I could see was being born in the wrong place with the wrong color skin.

"So, who are you looking for?" Jacob asked.

Bourland thought for a moment before answering. He squinted, staring into the distance as if he might see a lone rider.

"Figured perhaps the negro was too easy with his confession. That perhaps he'd had an accomplice he was trying to protect. Woodrow was stabbed with a big knife judging from what was left of him. But the slave didn't have a knife on him big enough for those cuts." He looked at Ma's pallid face apologetically.

"He might have lost the knife," I said.

"Maybe. But Garcia here is part Apache and he looked at the sign around the gulch and spotted another set of prints. Another man had mounted up and ridden south."

I couldn't breathe. Ma glanced at me.

"That could have been anybody," she said. "Maybe someone saw the wagon, rode up to investigate, then saw there was nothing to be done for the man."

"Maybe," Bourland said. "All I know is that you can never trust a negro, so when we found the sign, we headed off in pursuit."

"And the tracks led here? To our ranch?" The color had returned to Ma's cheeks now.

"We lost 'em down by the creek that runs across your land."

"Well, whoever it was, we haven't seen them, but I'll be sure to tell Charles to keep an eye out. The hands too."

"Thank you, ma'am," said the sheriff. "Figure we'll give up the chase now anyway. You're probably right. It could be anybody, and we already caught the black-hearted fella who did for old Woodrow. Truth be told nobody much liked the old buzzard. Besides, we didn't come equipped to travel far."

The small man looked relieved.

"That is a capital decision, sheriff," he said. "Just capital."

None of the men acknowledged he had spoken.

The sheriff thanked Ma again for the coffee and biscuits. Then the men mounted up and set off at a lope in the direction of town. We watched as they rode away, dust hazing the hot air behind them.

The elation I had felt at getting away with the killing had

evaporated as quickly as piss in the desert. A cloak of sorrow descended over me and I didn't dare look at Ma or Jacob. I watched the riders until they were just specks on the horizon, blurred by the distance and the heat. I thought of Hannibal's somber face and knew Sheriff Bourland was wrong. A man's skin says nothing about his honor. I'd barely known Hannibal and my actions had led to his untimely end, and yet he had kept his word to me. That told me all I needed to know.

When at last I looked away, Ma was staring at me with a strange expression on her pretty face. I cuffed at my eyes.

"Damn, that sun's bright," I said.

Ma said nothing.

"I think I'll ride out to tell Pa about the sheriff," I said, striding towards the corral for Buttermilk. As I saddled him, I caught myself wondering how long until I could get back into town to see Pearl.

But there was something else I needed to do first. I'd dig up that Colt Walker and get some practice in. No point in packing a lead pusher if I didn't know how to shoot.

WANT TO READ MORE?

If you enjoyed this novella and would like to read more about Jed White, he is a major character in the full-length novel, *Dark Frontier*, set in Oregon, 1890.

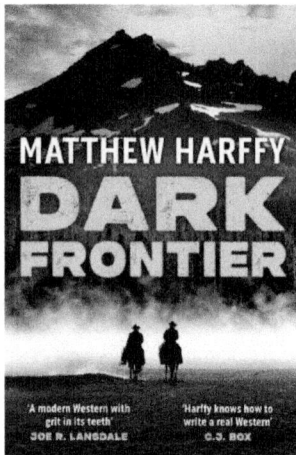

Find *Dark Frontier* in all good bookstores. It is available in hardback, paperback, e-book and audio.

INTERVIEW WITH THE AUTHOR

This interview about the novel, *Dark Frontier*, first appeared on 21st June 2024 on *Rock, Paper, Swords! – The Historical Action and Adventure Podcast*, that Matthew Harffy co-hosts with fellow author, Steven A. McKay. It has been edited here for clarity.

Steven A. McKay: What's the new book, *Dark Frontier*, about and why did you want to write it?

Matthew Harffy: Well, I'll read a little snippet of the blurb: "A thrilling historical Western set in 1890s Oregon."
And it says from the author of the critically acclaimed Benicia Chronicles. (I don't know who critically acclaimed them!)
"An English soldier turned policeman escapes to the American West for a new future. But life on the frontier proves far harder than he ever imagined. A man can flee from everything but his own nature."
And then it goes on to a bit more about the plot, but basically the story is about a soldier in 1890 who has then become a policeman. This guy, Lieutenant Gabriel Stokes, he's left the Metropolitan Police in London 1890 and he decides to

head to pastures new, leaving his terrible life behind him, and all the different stuff that's happened to him.

So as usual, a troubled back story, which is always great for a hero.

And he heads west to Oregon to go and visit a friend who he'd known in the army when they'd fought in the 2nd Anglo Afghan war together.

When he arrives at the very beginning of the book, he discovers there's been a murder and he gets embroiled in looking for the killer and trying to unearth what's going on. And there's lots of danger and thrills and spills, and of course, there's gunplay and fighting and all sorts along the way.

And Gabriel Stokes discovers, as it says, a man can flee from everything but his own nature.

Steven: Nice, but what about the second part of the question? Why did you want to write this?

Matthew: Because I've always loved Westerns. Really since I was a teenager. I used to love Western movies, probably even as a kid. But I started reading novels in my teenage years.

I remember when I was in my late teens and I got given *Lonesome Dove* by an American friend when I was living in Spain. And that's when I first read the massive tome that is *Lonesome Dove*. It must have been about '88 or '89, something like that. It won the Pulitzer Prize in '86 and it's a fantastic book. And that really just switched me on to Westerns then. And I started to pick up every book that I could find, every novel and non-fiction book as well.

And one of the things I was most depressed about when moving back from Spain, apart from having to leave our dogs behind, which was hugely traumatic - that was the most traumatic thing.

But the second most traumatic thing was having to leave lots of books behind and get rid of books before we left because we didn't have enough money to transport them.

And over the previous ten years, I'd bought not only a lot

of Western novels, but loads of non-fiction books about the Wild West and the history of the American West. So I've been sort of rebuilding that collection over the last few years.

I always wanted to write a Western. My best friend in Spain actually reminded me that the first book I started to write was a Western. And he reminded me that it was the first thing I'd ever really, really taken seriously, even though I only wrote a chapter or something!

Over the years, I got increasingly nervous about doing it. I've definitely got impostor syndrome about writing in general. I often feel I'm not really good enough to write a book. You know, who's going to want to read my book, even though obviously people do and have read a lot of my books, but you still sort of worry about it.

And then I think once you've carved out a niche in an area of fiction in a genre like we have in historical fiction, it's then that the imposter syndrome kicked in even more. Thinking about shifting to a slightly different genre or a totally different time frame in an era that's got guns and there's a lot more technology and it's a place that I've never lived. I felt very worried about doing it.

In the end I decided I'd take the plunge.

But I would do this thing of having the conceit of the main character being an Englishman travelling to America, which I don't think gives me leeway to get things wrong, but it sort of gives that fish out of water situation so I can sort of learn with the character.

Steven: That kind of nicely brings me on to the second question. You've gone from the Dark Ages, where people travel by horse, if they were rich enough, and fought with sword, spear and shield, to a period where there are trains, newspapers, paid law men and guns.

How hard was it to separate the two periods in your head as you were writing?

Matthew: Well, that's an interesting one. I think obviously the technology, as you say, is very different. And it's not difficult to separate those things, because the technology that was available is much closer to what we've got now. So it's a case of just subtracting a few of the things we've got. But they have telegraphs, by 1890. You can communicate pretty much instantly. They've got letters, they've got steamboats, so they can travel across the Atlantic in a few days.

By this point you've got the transcontinental railroads, so you can get across America in three days. Whereas before 1860 or 1870 or something, when they joined up the railroads from the east to the west, it took people literally three months or even longer to get across from the east to the west coast.

The railroad made America a smaller place and made it easier to get places.

So you've got all of that and obviously guns and everything, which makes things quite different. But I think having said that, it is still a lawless land. Or seemingly lawless. There's quite a lot of lawlessness because it's so big and sparsely populated in many parts of the West of America.

Even though 1890 is the date that apparently the census for the first time said that there was no frontier. Suddenly the population density in the West was high enough that there really was deemed to be no unsettled land. But that's a bit of a misconception. In reality there were lots of areas of the West that were still quite uninhabited.

Steven: Even nowadays in Scotland and England, you go to the middle of nowhere, a small farmhouse, it's basically lawless, isn't it? Because if you're out in the middle of nowhere and you phone the police, by the time they get there you're probably dead if you've confronted someone dangerous.

So it's going to be even worse than that in America because there's no phone call to the police.

Matthew: Obviously, at this time it is very lawless. So if somebody dies in a ditch somewhere, it's pretty much the same as in the early medieval period in the they find a dead body. But then what?

Steven: There's a sheriff or the marshal or someone whose job it is to sort it out. But of course, he is just a guy on his own.

Matthew: Yeah, no forensics or anything like that. And he's also got to contend with the fact that everyone's armed to the teeth, so anyone that doesn't like him can just shoot him in the back.

Going back to the actual thing of how I separated the things. How did I make them different?

I think that most of my storytelling for the Anglo-Saxon books and the Viking Age and early medieval books, is actually like westerns.

They're very similar. It's good versus bad. There's some sort of conflict, there's potentially a crime or somebody needs to be brought to justice. And really I look at the kings of the medieval period as like the cattle barons of the Wild West. And they've got a group of warriors around them, or gunslingers in the West. And they own a town and they do what they want.

And they basically lorded it over everybody else, supposedly bringing some sort of peace and stability to the area. Very much like a warlord would do in early medieval Northumbria.

Steven: And when you've got that guy being corrupt and doing horrible things, then it's up to the warriors in our books in the early medieval period, or in this case, Gabriel Stokes, the ex-policeman to step in and try to save the day.

Matthew: There's actually a conflict within the story in that Stokes wants to bring people to justice. He's a policeman. You know, he's come from a very rigid society. Although there's lots of crime in London, he still wants to bring people to justice and he thinks that that's the way to do it.

He's been in the army, so he knows how to handle himself in a fight, but he doesn't just want to string the man up from the nearest tree. He wants to bring him to court and see justice done. There's a dichotomy between his perspective and that of some local people who believe that if they catch the culprit, they should just kill him.

Some think the best solution is simply to get rid of him. That conflict runs throughout the story, and you have to imagine that it doesn't all end peacefully—sometimes, circumstances force his hand.

You also mentioned the press, which plays a significant role in the storyline. This was the beginning of the tabloid press in the late 19th century—the 1870s and 1880s—particularly in London.

Gabriel Stokes was involved with the Metropolitan Police during the investigation of the Jack the Ripper murders. It's only mentioned as part of his backstory, but at the time, the tabloid press sensationalized the case. There were even suggestions that some journalists wrote letters to themselves, posing as Jack the Ripper to generate more intrigue.

It's widely accepted that this kind of thing did happen. I believe *The Express* had only just started publishing a few months before the Ripper murders, and while no one thinks they were involved in the crimes, they certainly capitalized on the story. Their readership reportedly increased by around 250,000 within a few months due to the scandalous letters being published.

The story references this, along with some fictionalized murders that Gabriel Stokes investigates alongside a journalist. This contributes to his backstory, particularly why he had to leave—he couldn't tolerate journalists writing sensationalized stories, upsetting victims' families, and exploiting tragedies.

Steven: I was thinking that Jack the Ripper must have been active around the same time and in London, so I was curious. I wouldn't have been able to resist weaving him into the background, just as you have.

I remember Richard Lee from the Historical Novel Society advising that real historical events should be incorporated as background to help ground readers in the period. That's exactly what Jack the Ripper does—just mentioning him immediately conjures an image of grimy, fog-filled London. It also contrasts nicely with America, which, while existing in the same time period, feels entirely different.

Matthew: Absolutely. Stokes has a varied background—first in the army, then as a policeman. Including Jack the Ripper helps set the scene, evoking those dark, smog-filled streets and shadowy alleyways.

But there's also a fictionalized child murder in the story, which is truly horrific. Investigating that case sends Stokes into a downward spiral, leading to alcoholism and the unraveling of his life. That murder is an amalgamation of two real-life cases from the 1850s or 1860s. One of them is the infamous case of Fanny Adams, which gave rise to the phrase "Sweet Fanny Adams".

I read about those cases, and they were truly horrific. Some people have this romanticized idea that the past was genteel—afternoon teas in pastoral England—but in reality, crime and brutality were rampant. Life held little value for certain people, and those who were mentally unhinged could act with impunity—unless they were caught.

Steven: Unless, of course, Sherlock Holmes was on the case.

Matthew: He even gets a mention! I realized during my research that Sir Arthur Conan Doyle was developing Holmes around this time. The first book was published in 1888 or 1889—very close to these events…

To hear the rest of the interview (or read the full transcript) head on over to the *Rock, Paper, Swords!* podcast episode available on all podcast platforms. Matthew and Steven go on to discuss the historical use of racially-charged language, and Matthew's extensive research that took him riding the high desert of Oregon and shooting black powder pistols for some hands-on experience of the weapons featured in the novel.

To keep up-to-date with Matthew Harffy's new releases and events, sign up to his Newsletter on www.matthewharffy.com